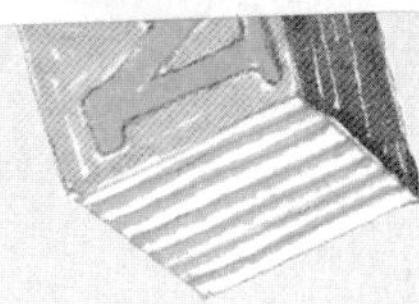

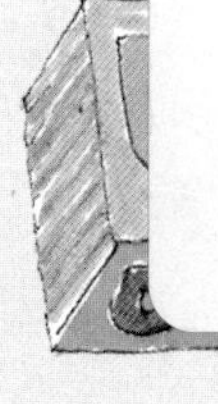

SOPHIE'S TERRIBLE TWOS

ROSEMARY WELLS

VIKING
An Imprint of Penguin Group (USA) Inc.

“How old is my Sophie this morning?”
asked Sophie’s mama.

Sophie knew how to say, “TWO!”
But she didn’t say it.
Sophie knew how to put up two fingers for “two years old.”
But she didn’t do it.

Because that was the day Sophie got up on the wrong side of the crib.

"Mama has a beautiful dress for her Sophie!"
said Mama.
"No pink!" said Sophie.

Daddy had sparkling fairy wings for Sophie.

But the fairy wings didn’t fly.

Daddy made Birthday Blueberry Pancakes for
Sophie, with two candles on top.
"So delicious!" said Mama.

But Sophie didn't like two things mixed together.
"No blueberries inside the pancakes!" said Sophie.

Ding dong! went the doorbell.
It was Granny.

Granny brought a big birthday present for Sophie.
Sophie unwrapped it.
Twenty-six Talking, Blinking Alphabet Blocks tumbled out.

“A!” “H!” “W!” sang the blocks.
“No more A B C!” said Sophie to the blocks.
“I know someone who has turned the corner onto
Grumpy Street,” said Mama.

Granny said, “Let’s hit the road!”

So Sophie got on her Push-Me-Pull-You Motorcycle.

Granny and Sophie went very fast,
weaving in and out of traffic.

They stopped in the Learning Curve Toy Shop to see
if there was a birthday present waiting there for Sophie.

But Sophie didn't want any more red, blue, or yellow.
She didn't want to hear Sounds of Favorite Farm Animals.
She didn't want to solve any more shape puzzles.

Granny had an inspiration.
"How about a saber-toothed tiger suit?" said Granny.
"Five yesses!" said Sophie.

So they went over to Zeke's Palace of Costumes.
"Have you got a saber-toothed tiger suit in size 2?"
Granny asked Zeke.
Zeke had one size 2 tiger suit left in the back room.

The tiger suit fit just right.
It had fiery eyes, dripping fangs,
and enormous claws on glittery feet.

"Look out! Everyone hide!"
shouted the people on the street.

Mama and Daddy opened the front door.
"Oh no!" shouted Daddy. "A saber-toothed tiger!"
"Right here in our house!" squeaked Mama.

"It's only me!" said Sophie.
"How old is that terrible tiger?" asked Granny.

Sophie held up two claws.
"Terrible Two!" said Sophie.

For Frances Wells Arms

VIKING
An imprint of Penguin Young Readers Group
Published by the Penguin Group
Penguin Group (USA)
375 Hudson Street
New York, New York 10014, U.S.A.

USA / Canada / UK / Ireland / Australia / New Zealand / India / South Africa / China
Penguin Books Ltd, Registered Offices: 80 Strand, London WC2R 0RL, England

For more information about the Penguin Group visit www.penguin.com

First published in the United States of America by Viking, an imprint of Penguin Young Readers Group, 2014

LIBRARY OF CONGRESS CATALOGING-IN-PUBLICATION DATA
Wells, Rosemary.
Sophie's terrible twos / by Rosemary Wells.
pages cm
Summary: On her second birthday, Sophie gets up on the wrong side of the crib and behaves terribly until her grandmother has an inspiration.
ISBN 978-0-670-78512-4 (hardcover)
[1. Behavior—Fiction. 2. Family life—Fiction. 3. Mice—Fiction. 4. Birthdays—Fiction.] I. Title.
PZ7.W46843Sop 2014
[E]—dc23
2013014733

Manufactured in China
The art for this book was created using ink, watercolor, and gouache.

3 5 7 9 10 8 6 4 2

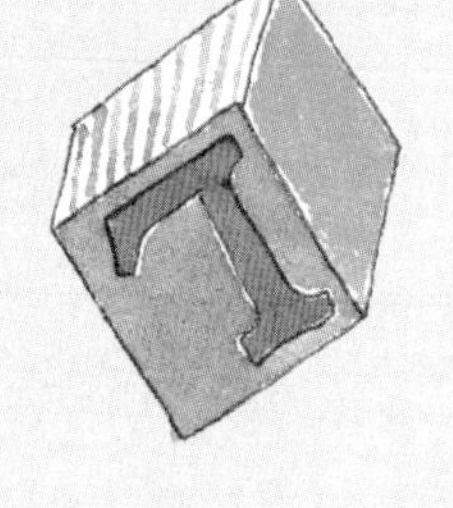